PLASTIC BAGS & PAPER HEARTS

The Stock Boy's Daddy

Daniel Elijah Sanderfer

Mountain Ranch Publishing

To my inner little

PROLOGUE

STEVEN

Life has been a little hard on me. I'd thought by now that I would be someone... someone successful... someone loved... someone that mattered. However, I'm barely getting by. My name is Steven, and I live in a little town in the Appalachian Mountains called Jonesville. Don't get too excited. Although it's beautiful here, there isn't much to do. We have a country grocery store, a courthouse, a hardware store, a dollar general, and a Walmart. This town thought it was something else when Walmart decided to build here.

I work at the country grocery as a stock boy. It's owned by a sweet little old lady named Mrs. Grable. Her husband owns another branch of our little chain, in the next town over, called Pennington Gap. Pennington Gap is like New York City to the folks in Jonesville. They have a chain grocery store, a Walgreens, and a hand full of chain restaurants. It's not glamorous but it's home to the mountain folk that reside here.

I was born and raised here, but I was never

able to put down roots due to being passed around the foster system most of my life. You see, my real parents weren't the best people. Daddy was a drunk who slept around on mama the whole time they were together, and mama was distant. I don't remember a lot about her. Growing up, I mostly kept to myself and didn't bother asking her for anything. You were lucky to pull her away from the TV long enough to make dinner, much less do something motherly. Dinner was just usually something she could microwave.

I think she just gave up on life... much like a lot of people here. They've resigned themselves to a mundane existence of getting by until someone puts em' in the ground. I don't want to live like that. I'd like to make enough someday to buy a nice place up in the hills, maybe with some land. Yeah, get a couple of cows, maybe a chicken or two. That would be the life... but I ain't holding my breath until it happens. Mrs. Grable says one day my ship will come. She says I'm handsome and bright with a great personality despite my circumstances.

She's been my biggest supporter since she hired me just out of school. I'm not even sure why I finished, but I guess it kept me out of trouble and gave me something to do. Her husband doesn't speak much. He's kind of a reserved older man who doesn't care for people my age. Still, I treat him with the utmost respect. Mrs. Grable says he likes me, he really does, he just doesn't have much to say. I'm the total opposite... I have so much to say and no one in the world to say it to.

I normally work six days a week from 7 a.m. until closing time at 7 p.m. It helps me pay the rent at the motor lodge where I live. It's just across the street from the grocery store, so I don't need a car. I just walk wherever I need to go and Mrs. Grable is always giving me food close to the expiration date to help tie me over until payday. Mr. Grable doesn't know, but I'm eternally grateful for her charity. It's not a great life, but I have everything I need. My only day off is Sunday when the Grable's go to church and spend time with family. So, life goes in a small town.

I lived with them for a short time when I turned eighteen and aged out of the foster system. They were nice enough to let me stay in their basement until I got paid and could get a room at the lodge. The owners of the lodge are nice enough. They appreciate a long-term paying tenant in a town like this. Most nights, they're lucky to get one or two weary truckers or travelers who have no choice but to stop due to exhaustion.

A few times, I thought about hitching a ride with one of the truckers and leaving everything behind, but something keeps me here. It's almost as if the fates have conspired for me to stay until whenever something happens. I'm not sure what that is, but I suppose I would miss this place if I ever did leave. Anyways, you're probably tired of hearing my sad story so I'll carry on. I turn my gaze to the mountains in the distance as the rain gently falls on the parking lot outside. This place is always deserted in the evening.

Sometimes I get lost thinking about all the families in their cozy homes up there… dad just getting in from work on the farm. Kids silently doing homework in their rooms. Mama making dinner in the kitchen. They don't know how lucky they are to have what they do. I'd give anything… anything to have a life like that; a place to call home, family, someone who loves me. Unfortunately, I don't… so I must carry on all by myself and pray that someday my ship will come.

With a ragged breath, I stand from the picnic table just outside the store and head toward the door. Mrs. Grable is just inside wiping down the checkout belt as I flash a smile and head back to the produce department to stock some more veggies. A quick glance out the window to our one stop light, I notice a U-Haul, pulling a car, waiting to turn. Who in their right mind would ever move to a place like this? I shrug and continue stocking my wares as the bell on the door jingles.

Mrs. Grable's voice breaks through the silence, "Evenin' how ya'll doin?"

I turn to see if who it is, and it's just a man.

Mrs. Grable calls everyone y'all, whether it's just one person or a family. It's A tall man with a fancy button-down shirt tucked into his jeans. He's a little scruffy and worn like the boots his jeans are tucked into. I lick my lips and swallow hard. I see guys like him every day. No one around here knows I'm gay, if they did, they'd hunt me down like some animal and kill me. Oh, what I'd give to spend one night with a big, strapping man like him and let him teach me what it means to feel love. I've never had anything to go on, that's why I don't say again. How is someone supposed to know what love is when they've never felt it before?

He grabs a basket from the rack and proceeds my direction. A faint heat invades my cheeks as I tuck a strand of my shaggy blonde hair behind my ear. He's standing right next to me... I can feel his presence, but I keep my head down. Part of me wants to speak, but I never can find my voice when a beautiful man is next to me. It all comes from my daddy. He used to cuss me like a dog and hit me if I dared to meet his gaze. So, I just keep my eyes down when I speak to anyone.

A soft finger on my shoulder, followed by a voice prompts me to mumble, "Can I help you?"

The gentleman replies, his voice is soft and friendly, "Would you mind telling me if y'all carry Milano cookies?"

"We sure do," I reply excitedly as I lift my gaze a little, "they're on aisle three."

"Thanks," he winked, "they're my favorite."

Inside, I just died a little. It was the first time I'd ever looked at someone's face. For a moment, I thought I'd gone blind. He looked young, but I could tell by the salt on the fringes of his pepper-black hair that he was much older than he looked. Maybe fifty-ish if I had to guess. Age never meant anything to me. There are good and bad people, both young and old. It's all a matter of perspective. If you go about life always expecting something bad to happen, then it most likely will. However, if you have a little faith that things might turn alright... maybe it will or maybe it won't. At least it makes life less difficult. It's like the old country song that always plays on the store radio, "Keep on the sunny side of life..."

JACK

It felt strange to be in a country grocery store. Back where I'm from, there are supercenters every-where, open twenty-four hours a day, seven days a week. I figured I better stop in before this place shuts down for the night. I imagine there aren't too many shops in a place like this.

My name is Jack, and life has been a little hard on me lately. I had a good job, a good life, a nice house, and a loyal wife. Unfortunately, I threw that all away for a hookup. Before you start hating me, hear me out. There would never be another woman in my life besides Kate, but the truth is we should have never married at all. You see, I'm gay, always have been and always will be. Getting married didn't change that, it just masked it. No one else knew that until Kate found me in our den gettin' blown off by the lawn boy.

She, of course, freaked out and after the lawn boy was gone, she let me have it. "How long has this been going on? Is he the first or have there been more?" The list goes on. Most importantly, I was sure to let her know that it had nothing to do with her looks. She's a beautiful gal of forty-eight. She never had to deal with the baggage of excess weight from children because she couldn't. Also, she went power walking every morning with our neighbor, Gale.

So, why, of all places, did I choose to come to a place like Jonesville, Virginia after the divorce. Well, I grew up here. Years ago, when mama and daddy were still alive, they owned a farm out here and taught my sister and me all the basics of rural living. When we got older, daddy got a job in Johnson City and we sold the farm and moved away. I've always hated city life, and I vowed if I ever got the chance I would come back here... back to my roots. Now, that I ain't got anybody to stay in the city for, I packed up all my stuff that Kate didn't get in the divorce and headed this way.

I came up here a few weeks ago to lick my wounds and recover from breaking her heart. It honestly hurt me as much as it did her because if I'd have just been honest with myself in the first place, we wouldn't have wasted thirty years of our lives trying to make something work that was doomed from the beginning. Anyways, while I was down here I decided to look at a few places and found one all to itself in the mountains, not too far from mama and daddy's old farm.

The original house is gone now, but the people who bought the land built a nice ranch on the property and are still operating it the way daddy used to. I'm a little too old to start a farm, but I've made enough in my life as a car salesman to live well for a while. In fact, all Kate really wanted was the house and a vehicle. She's worked as a bank teller for about as long as I was a car salesman, so money wasn't her biggest concern. She's got a 401K and savings that would make a stockbroker wet his pants.

I think the thing I'll miss the most is the company. When you've lived with someone for that long, you kind of get used to their presence, and despite the bitter way things ended we decided to still stay friends. She was much calmer when she realized I wasn't having some midlife crisis and just wanted to try dudes for a spell. One of the saddest things about our relationship was how we deprived one another of intimacy. I, of course, couldn't help that I really wished she was a man. But, when she was told by the doctor that she'd never be able to have children, she stopped caring about intimacy altogether.

It's weird, we may have slept in the same bed in the same room for all this time, but there was nothing but ice between us. I can't tell you how many times I laid there wishing it was some cute young guy sleeping next to me instead of her. I even got up, when desires got too overwhelming, and jerked off to porn in the bathroom. What a sad, sad, life for us both. No desire for women on my part, and no desire for anything on hers. I tried to tell her that a woman's lot in life isn't about bearing children. She'd hear none of it. I knew it was something she had always wanted desperately and just couldn't have.

When sex was out of the question, she wanted to adopt, but I never really wanted children to begin with. I just wanted to do what I was supposed to do in the eyes of society. Unfortunately, conformity is the enemy of happiness. Everything eventually just becomes so mundane and routine that you can about set your watch to the events of the day. Breakfast, rush to get ready, work, get home, dinner, then bedtime by ten. Thank God I don't have to endure it anymore.

While I browsed the aisles of the humble country grocery, I couldn't get my mind off the cute blonde stock boy working up front. Shit, what I'd give to throw caution to the wind and ask if he'd be interested in a romp. I knew better though in a town like this. People don't take too kindly to "alternative" lifestyles around here. I'd already scouted Grindr to see if there was anybody around, but it was mostly older gentlemen. I've always had an appetite for young guys myself.

I guess part of me is still just a young curious boy who wants to explore the things that make us beautiful with other young curious boys. I turned my gaze to him again and watched him bend over to get another box of tomatoes. Damn, that ass was the stuff all-night wank sessions were made of. I bet it was hairless and hard as granite. I bet his hole was pink and as tight as a drum. I closed my eyes momentarily and pictured it begging to be bred by my uncut cock.

I stuck my hand in my pocket to adjust myself and carried on. I needed to get to the new house before nightfall. I wasn't too sure about these roads around here, and the last thing I wanted was to get lost in this wilderness. On my way to the register, the elderly woman leaned toward her microphone, "Bagger please?"

I watched from across the store as he rushed to her command. "Did ya find everything you need, sir?"

"For right now," I smiled.

Momentarily, I caught the stock boy staring at me and winked again. He looked so nervous and unsure about himself. He didn't say anything, but as I paid for my groceries and went to pick up the bags he grabbed them and announced, "I've got em, sir. It's all part of our customer service."

I met the old woman's gaze and grinned, "How nice."

She nodded proudly, "That's just the way we do things around here." She handed me a receipt with change, then crooned, "Have a blessed day."

The young stock boy was waiting for me just outside the store. We stood for a moment in silence before he asked, "Which one's yours?"

I pointed to the U-Haul and he proceeded. The rain was still coming down, so I made haste to get to the passenger's side and open the door so he could put them in. Once he was done, I passed him a five-dollar bill and smiled, "Thanks."

"Your welcome," he bowed before sprinting back to the store. Oh, what I'd given for just a moment more with him. That hard body, those luscious lips. I knew what I'd be doing tonight once I got settled in... getting lost in a simulated dream of making love all night long with that sweet country angel, what was his name, ah yes, Steven.

The next morning when I woke up, I fixed

myself a cup of coffee and got lost daydreaming as I stood on the balcony overlooking the forest. I didn't really have much to do outside of unpacking, but I wanted so bad to head back down to the store and see if I see the stock boy again. Maybe if I were careful, I could snap a picture with my phone so I could stare at his beautiful face and body more.

PLASTIC BAGS & PAPER HEARTS

DANIEL ELIJAH SANDERFER

ONE

STEVEN

I awoke to the sun peeking through the dated curtains of my room. I'd been up for a while now thinking about the future... wondering if I'd ever make it out of this god-forsaken place. It wouldn't take me long to get ready. Most of the time, I just threw on the jeans and t-shirt I wore the day before. Every day it's all the same, I roll out of bed and cross the room to open the curtains and let the sunshine in. For a moment, I look around to see what's going on in the world.

A few cars are usually moving about... people who work in the city and stop at the gas station for a quick fill-up and coffee before going about their way. I grab my wallet and sweater, then start the walk across the street to my job. My whole world exists within a one-block radius. Sometimes I gaze at the horizon and wonder what it's like beyond the few hundred feet of roadway I see in either direction.

My mind momentarily drifted to the man I saw yesterday. I bet he has a nice house, probably a wife and kids. I couldn't imagine a sexy older guy like him being single. He seemed interested in me from the way he winked, but one can never be too sure. When I had a phone, I would sometimes hop on Grindr to try and find someone to kill my loneliness with. Oftentimes, I'd find a daddy or two, but they were usually married and looking to fool around behind their wife's back. I may not be worth very much, but I'll be damned if I'm going to be the other person in a relationship. How am I supposed to build a future with someone who already has a life?

There was an older widowed farmer who used to pick me up sometimes after work, but it's been a long time since I've seen him in the store. I worry that something may have happened to him. As you know, I don't have a car, or I'd go check on him. I can only hope he's staying away due to this whole COVID-19 thing. We didn't really do much other than hold and kiss, but he made me feel special… like a little boy does with his Grandpa. Sometimes we'd just sit on his porch and I would listen to him tell me stories about the old days when he was young.

That's the kind of life I want again, a life of peace and happiness. Sittin' out on the porch until dark and just talking about nothing at all… holding onto each other by the fireplace and letting the feelings of warmth and stability envelop me. When I was a little boy, I used to pray for a daddy that loved me. That prayer is still the same, only the role has changed. The type of daddy I'm looking for is someone confident and strong. Someone who makes me feel safe and I swear to God I'll treat him the way a boy should. I'll fix his dinner, obey his every command, and in return, he'll reward me with sweet kisses and companionship for life.

I sigh as I walked into the store and grabbed my apron from under the checkout stand. Mrs. Grable is in her office doing paperwork as she glances over her glasses and smiles, "Good Morning, Steven."

"Morning, Mrs. Grable."

"Could you work on the can food rows today? We need to turn the stock; old Ms. Harmon got a can of expired beans the other day and she'll never let us live it down if she doesn't see some changes around here."

"Yes, ma'am," I reply respectfully before reporting to my post.

I always like rotating stock. I can just get lost in the music and toss the cans close to expiration in a big shopping cart. Mrs. Grable usually puts a big discount sign on them and people flock to the store in hopes of getting a deal. Word travels fast around here. Not even ten minutes after I wheel the cart to the front, the old farmer's wives come-a-runnin' to stock up their pantries. They don't pay no mind to a can that's set to expire in a couple of days. It's not the food has gone bad; it's just we can't sell it past the date on the can.

The day was going by pretty fast when Mrs. Grable made a round and spotted me obsessively turning all the remaining cans to where their labels were facing forward. "I've always loved your attention to detail, Steven."

I smiled at her, "It's just the way I am."

"I know," she nods. "Why don't you go take your break? We're pretty slow right now."

"Okay."

With my hands in my pockets, I made my way out of the store and took a seat at the old picnic table out front. I love to just sit and watch the people go by on the road. At the stoplight, I could see someone turning into the parking lot. It figures, every time I take a break, we get busy.

Upon further inspection, I recognized the person driving as the man from yesterday. I suddenly felt nervous and my stomach flip-flopped as he stepped out of his Buick. I bit my bottom lip and held my breath as he removed his sunglasses and tucked them into the front pocket of his shirt. His snug-fitting khakis were making me weak. The longer I stared, I couldn't help but notice the outline of his cock imprinted in the supple fabric. Dear God, what I'd give to be on my knees in front of that bulge worshipping it.

He caught me staring from across the lot and tossed up a hand, "Taking a break, kiddo?"

"Yeah," I grinned.

Him calling me kiddo made my dick twitch in my pants. I'd always dreamed someone would call me that. Often when I'm dreaming of daddies and whacking off at night, I think of them calling me that. In my visions, I'm lying on my belly with them inside of me. I can feel the weight of their body on my back. I can feel their strong arms wrapped around me, telling me that I'm such a good boy... such a sweet boy. I reply breathlessly, "Yes daddy... make me your boy... your property... your one and only."

I crossed my legs as he approached and took a seat next to me, "Whatcha doin?"

"Just watching the world go by."

Silence lingered for a moment before he extended a hand, "I'm Jack, by the way."

"Steven..."

We shook then separated. He was playing with his fingers as he stared in the direction of the road and continued, "So... you been working here long?"

"Since I graduated high school."

He chuckled, "Well from the way you look, that couldn't have been too long ago."

I turn to him and grin, "Not too long... about a year or two ago."

For a moment, we held our gaze and searched one another. He was trying to ask me silent questions and I was trying to answer him. I've done this dance before with other curious men in the store. It usually ended up with us sneaking off to the bathroom for a quickie. In this case, I still had some time left on my break and I was more than happy to oblige if I was what he had a hankering for. Call it my extra effort toward providing the best customer service I possibly can.

In those tension-filled moments, I took note that he wasn't wearing a wedding ring. A quick shift of my leg, pressed it against the side of his and he smiled, "Forgive me if I'm wrong, but are you?"

My eyes twinkled as I replied, "I can be anything you want me to be... daddy."

He bit his lip and sucked in a breath through his nose. Then, with a quick pat to my knee, he stood and mumbled, "Maybe some other time... I need to get back to the house. I'm expecting a call for a potential job."

I was disappointed, but I wasn't about to burn a bridge that was so few and far between, so I flirtatiously replied, "Well... my offer still stands. Just name the place and time."

"I'll keep that in mind," he winked before heading into the store and left me there with a raging boner and forlorn desires for company. Damn him for getting my hopes up. Damn him for being so attractive and receptive. I guess it'd be another lonely night of hugging my pillow and wishing it were someone... anyone to make me feel human again.

JACK

I needed to get into the store fast. Hopefully, to God, they had a bathroom where I could adjust myself because I was hard as a rock after that little encounter. Everything was a blur as I searched for signs and managed to find an arrow pointing toward the back of the store. The elderly woman who runs the place tossed up a hand and shouted, "How y'all doin' today?"

"Fine," I mumbled hurriedly and retreated to the safety of the men's room. Inside the stall, I unleashed my erection and groaned with desire. God, I wanted him... I wanted him so bad I could practically feel his tight hole around my cock. It was everything I could do to keep from stroking it right there, but I tucked it tighter into my briefs and zipped myself back up. On the way out, I met Steven going in and he squinted at me with a curious expression. That sweet baby face was the stuff wet dreams were made of. Last night, I dreamt of him on his knees, his supple and full lips wrapped around the head of my cock, and those eyes begging to know if he was doing it right.

What I'd give to be that direction in his life... to be the one who made him feel ecstasy beyond his wildest dreams. I may be older, but I've been around the block and one thing I pride myself on is making boys feel good. I grabbed a hand towel and my thoughts trailed off. I'd make him feel good alright. I'd make him feel things he'd never felt before and he'd do the same. There was something so innocent and pure about him. He wasn't spoiled like city boys. He was just... adorable. The kind of boy you spend forever with... not just a one-night stand.

When our moment did come, I want it to be special. Not just some emotionless act committed in a heated rush. No, I wanted to spend time with him. I wanted to show him how beautiful he was by worshipping every inch of his young body... treat him like the country prince he is.

I didn't really need anything from the store, but a bottle of cheap wine and some crackers wouldn't hurt. So, I made a selection and hurried out of the store, but rest assured I would be back tomorrow to visit him again.

STEVEN

At the end of the day, I still couldn't stop thinking about Jack. Mrs. Grable was pulling out at the light in front of the store as I headed in the direction of the Motor Lodge. As I passed the gas station, a familiar voice shouted out from the gas pump, "Hey... Steven!"

I scanned my surroundings. Occasionally, one of my old foster moms or dads would see me at the grocery and say hello. It always felt kind of weird for someone you lived with to talk to you like some kind of old friend. In my mind, it's just a reminder that I wasn't good enough for them to make me a permanent member of their family. Those things can mess a kid up pretty good and leave you with so many unanswered questions. Was there something wrong with me? Did I do something to make me unworthy of their love?

I shook my head to snap myself out of it and permitted my eyes to see who it was. When I did, my heart stopped... it was Jack... in all of his masculine beauty. "Can I give you a ride?"

I stopped and smiled as I turned my gaze to my feet, "I appreciate it, but I'm just walking to the motor lodge next door."

He glanced that direction, then arched a brow, "You live at the motor lodge?"

"It's a long story," I sighed.

He waved in dismissal, "No judgment, you don't have to explain. Well... since I can't drive you home, what do you say to dinner?"

I lifted my eyes and met his gaze. His eyes looked so kind and hopeful. How could I say no? It wasn't like I had anything else to do. He continued talking nervously as he waited for my answer, "I know there's not a lot of places around here, but we could grab a burger and eat it in the car, or we could go up to the pizza place and grab something."

As much as I wanted to, I didn't have any money. So, I politely kept walking toward the lodge, "I wish I could, but I don't have any money."

He looked slightly offended as he stepped away from his car and walked closer to me, "What kind of person offers to take someone to dinner then doesn't pay?"

"I-I'm not sure."

He shook his head, "The question was, would you like to go to dinner with me? Not would you like to buy dinner?"

A faint smile formed on my lips as I attempted to divert the question again, "I was just going to have a sandwich or something when I get back to my room. You don't have to spend your money on me."

He stretched out his hand and rested it on my shoulder, "But I want to, kiddo. You know... you don't have to be so afraid to make eye contact with me. I'd never hurt anyone... especially someone as precious as you."

I felt my cheeks sear with blush as I turned my gaze to the sky and exhaled, "Okay... geez... if you really want to, and you're sure I'm not putting you out then yes, I would love to have dinner with you."

"Awesome," he grinned, before tousling my hair. I turned to follow him back to his car. When I got to the door, he rushed ahead and opened it for me. I wasn't sure what to say or do. His kindness had put me off my game immensely. Finally, after he'd finished pumping the gas, he hung the nozzle back up and got in.

I was glancing around, trying to take in all the sites of his fancy vehicle. It smelt like leather and men's cologne. I wanted to remember this smell because they should bottle it up and sell it as an aphrodisiac. With a gentle grip to my knee, he mumbled, "Buckle up, kiddo," then buckled his own belt and shifted the car into drive.

All was silent as we waited at the stop light at the intersection of the grocery store and gas station. Then, he broke it, "So, how was your day at the store?"

I wasn't used to talking to anyone much. Usually, the only person I talked to during the day were a handful of customers asking where something was or Mrs. Grable when she needed something. This was all so new and unfamiliar, but I couldn't deny how nice it was to not have to spend the next few hours or so chasing thoughts inside my head and trying to find something I haven't already watched on the old color CRT TV in my room.

"It was good," I managed to croak out before asking him the same question with a follow-up, "How did that call go from that job? Did you get it?"

He shrugged, "I gave it my best shot. The boss seemed to like my experience, but the drive is a little far to commute to from here."

"Where is it?"

"Middlesboro, just on the other side of the Cumberland Gap."

"Ah," I nodded.

Silence lingered for a minute again as we drove through downtown, and I couldn't help but notice a few little shops had opened since the last time I'd been up this way. The very last building on the left was the burger place. Jack pulled out front, then hopped out and asked, "What would you like? I don't think they have happy meals," he smirked.

I curled my lip, "Happy meals? I'm not six!"

He closed his eyes and shook his head, still amused with his own joke. Inside my mind, I kind of wish they did. I used to love the little cars they'd give out and would spend hours just staring into oblivion while pushing it across the ledge of the car window. Then, when I'd get home, I'd take it everywhere with me. I never got many toys in foster care, so each one I cherished and would panic when any would turn up missing. When you have so little, to begin with, you try to hold on to what little things you do have.

My silence prompted Jack to ask again, "I'll get you anything you want, just tell me."

"Would a cheeseburger and fries be okay? Nothing too expensive!"

He shook his head, "Don't worry about the money, I just want you to be happy and enjoy yourself."

As I stared at him in the line to order our food, I couldn't help but get lost in the way his khakis accentuated his butt. Occasionally, he would shift his weight which made his butt look firmer, and I, well, I just sank into the seat and sighed a dreamy sigh or forlorn desire. It didn't take too long before he was back with two paper sacks slightly discolored from grease.

He passed one to me, then sat the other between us before checking the road and pulling out. "Know anywhere nice we could sit while we eat these?"

I glanced inside and scanned the contents curiously. I've always been a little picky. The brief thought that there better not be any mustard on there crossed my mind before I answered his question, "Um yeah, there's a little park when you turn right up the next street. It's not very big, but there's never anyone up there and it has great views of the town."

"Alright then," he crooned, "that's where we'll go. Oh… by the way, I got you something at the burger stand."

"What?" I said as my eyes lit up.

From within the breast pocket of his shirt, he pulled out a tiny red car. I almost started to cry as he explained, "Just for references, they do have happy meals, but I told them I just wanted the toy."

He handed it to me and smiled, "It's for you."

I was speechless as I brought it to my chest and mumbled, "Thank you."

He pulled into a spot in the park then turned to me. With a playful grip to my knee, he grinned and replied, "Your welcome, kiddo."

Kiddo, there was that word again. The one that made me weak in the knees and in the crotch. Moving on from the moment, we unpacked our food and just watched the sun set behind the hills and buildings of our little country town while we ate. In the back of my mind, he would never know what that little car meant to me. Also, when I got home, I would definitely put it with my other ones from when I was a little boy.

Sometimes, I wish I were a little boy again. I miss the days when I could hide under my bed and play with my car while my stepparents fought in the background. It was safe there... all alone in my little world where no one could find me and hurt me ever again. Maybe that's why I stay here in this little town... because it feels safe. Out there in the city, people are mean and cruel and I know all too well how badly people can hurt you.

Although, it seems as hard as I tried to hide away from people, someone still found me, and I have a feeling he's not going to leave me anytime soon. The problem is, how do I learn to trust someone? How do I know he won't eventually leave me like everyone else in my life did?

I'd been mechanically chewing my burger as

I pondered all these different scenarios. Then, like the answer to a silent prayer, he turned to me and chuckled. "You've got ketchup all over your little chin."

I glanced around for a napkin, but before I could find one he leaned in and wiped it off himself, "There," he smiled.

Something inside my heart just snapped. When he touched my chin, I traveled back in time to those moments when I'd pray by the bedside for a daddy who could wipe away all of my tears. Okay, so maybe it wasn't a tear, but it was close, and he made me feel something for the first in years. He made me feel like someone really cared about me.

After dinner, Jack drove me back to my room and even walked me to the door. His hands were in his pockets as were mine as we stared off the tiny balcony at the darkness all around us. "I had a nice time tonight."

His voice was low and sweet and I could feel each syllable of his words vibrate in my chest. "So did I," I replied meekly.

"Maybe, if it's not too much trouble we could do this again tomorrow night?"

"I'd like that."

As I lifted my eyes to meet his, I could see the

reflection of the stars inside of his eyes. A look of wonder and amazement graced my expression. He looked like some superhero standing there haloed in the soft streetlight. A faint hint of honeysuckle was in the air from a nearby pasture. He slowly extended his hand and tucked a wayward strand of hair behind my ear. Then with a fatherly smile, he leaned in to kiss my forehead, "Goodnight, kiddo."

I didn't reply. Inside of my mind, fireworks were exploding like the night sky on the fourth of July. In silence, he walked down the stairs then out to his car. From the balcony, I propped my chin in my hands and watched him back out. That's when I had a childish thought. I whispered under my breath, if there's something here, then he'll look back up and wave at me. I was about to turn around and go inside, when to my surprise he paused, then lifted his gaze, smiled, and waved.

I waved back like a little boy waves at his father heading off to work in the morning, then when he was out of sight my fingers folded into a little fist and I brought it up to my heart. I'd keep his tender waves and kiss with me for when the night got too lonely. At least now I knew there was someone else out there and maybe... just maybe... he was thinking about me too.

JACK

On the drive home, I zoned out and was lost

thinking about Steven. Something happens when I'm around him that I can't explain it, and I'm still not sure whether it's right for me to feel this way. When I'm around him, I feel so protective and fatherly. It's like something inside of my soul knows he needs someone to watch over him. I know he's a grown boy and has lived on his own, way longer than I have, but it just doesn't seem fair. Boys like him need an older friend to give them advice and guide them through the winding roads of life.

I wasn't sure how I got from the motor lodge to my house, but as I sat in the driveway, I wished so much that I could be holding him tonight. He just seems so sad, vulnerable, and alone. Look at me, I've never been a father, although there were times when I was younger I wished I had some little guy who looked up to me.

It'd be another night filled with sweating through my sheets and fantasizing about him on his knees in front of me or sitting in my lap as we kissed and I gently rocked him back and forth on my cock. God, what is wrong with me? I need to taste him soon. I needed to know if his body felt as good wrapped around mine as I dream it would.

TWO

STEVEN

The next day at work, I kept the little car Jack gave me in my pocket and would occasionally take it out to look at it. Every time the door would open, I would hope that it was him walking in to rescue me. I couldn't wait to see Jack again. I knew it was like something out of a Disney movie, but it had become my motivation for getting out of bed in the morning. The day went on without any signs of him, where was he? By closing time my heart was breaking. All those questions from my childhood were starting to surface again. Did I do something wrong? Why doesn't he like me? He said, why don't we meet again tomorrow. Where is he?

On the walk back to the motor lodge, I realized that I had to pee so bad I couldn't stand it. I'd never make it to the room in time, and the lady at the gas station would call the cops if I came running in there like a lunatic. Oh no, I could feel it coming. I crossed my legs and paused for a minute. Why me? I used to wet myself when I was little because I was too afraid to ask to go to the bathroom in class. However, this had nothing to do with fear. I could have gone to the bathroom any time before Mrs. Grable closed, but I was too preoccupied with my thoughts about Jack to do so. I kept thinking all day, where is Jack?

Once I gained the confidence that I wasn't going to wet myself, I made haste to my room. No sooner than I got inside and closed the door, I could feel the front of my pants getting warmer, then gently slide down my leg. Oh no... I didn't make it. But... something felt strangely good about being so warm and wet. I was actually getting harder and harder by the second as I undid my pants then plopped down on the bed. It was almost orgasmic. At the relief of the pressure on my waist, I felt another stream pulse from my cock right into the front of my undies, soaking them completely.

I drifted back and started to moan at the sensation. Why did it feel so good? When I was all done, I started to stroke myself and dream about Jack. He'd smile and say, "Did my kiddo wet himself? Does daddy need to change him?"

Then, he'd feel up my crotch and whisper, right in my ear, "You're so wet." With, one hand on my cock jerking away, the other one was drifting up my chest and making circles around my nips. I pinched the left one a little and caught my breath in my throat. The sensation sent a jolt of electricity up my cock shaft. It wasn't long before I could feel my love rising ever higher. I was going to explode.

I turned my gaze to my dick and moaned, "Why does this feel so good?"

My muscles tensed and my throat closed. I was holding onto every shred of control I had to keep from erupting like a volcano all over myself. Then without warning, I exhaled with a heavy moan, I shot wave after wave of sweet love all over my tummy. In the silence of the room, all that remained was the shutters of my breath and the buzz of the fluorescent light in the bathroom. I was so close; I could have made it if I wanted to... but I chose not to. A sinister smile formed on my lips. I'd been a bad boy and it felt so damn good. Now I need to get my wet clothes into some water to clean them up as well as clean all the love off my skin. Maybe it is a perfect time to take a shower in my clothes. Did I do this because I missed Jack? Was I turning into a little boy again, unable to control my body functions just because I missed him so much? If, I ever see him again, will I tell him about it? Where is Jack? The water cascading over my soiled body and clothes feels so good, but not as good as his touch.

JACK

Just as I thought, I couldn't sleep. Why had I gotten so busy that time flew by and I missed going and taking Steven out to dinner again? I'd changed positions a hundred times, but every time I closed my eyes all I could see was his beautiful face. I had messed up, I needed to see him again. Finally, I jumped up and crossed the room. There wasn't any air circulating through the open bedroom window. I stood there for a moment gazing out into the darkness as beads of sweat traced their way down my body. I couldn't take this anymore.

In a heated rush, I grabbed my khakis and button-up shirt from the discarded pile on the floor. With a glance at the alarm clock on the nightstand, I grabbed my keys and wallet and made my way to the door. I was like a zombie with only one thing on my mind. His name just kept repeating over and over in my head like a scratched record. His face kept flashing in visions of light. I gripped my head and shouted, "Stop it, damnit! Stop it!"

As I lifted my gaze and stared out the screen door, I made a decision. I had to have him, I had to get to him and ease this aching in my heart and cock. I had to apologize for not seeing him today. Time be damned. It was a careful descent down the mountain. I wasn't used to driving these roads at night, but his heartbeat was like a beacon calling me. I could feel it in my chest, beating in sync with his dreams.

STEVEN

I rose up in bed and rubbed my eyes. I was

dreaming of Jack again. I was sitting in his lap while he read me a story. I was in my underwear and I could see his cock tented through the opening in his bathrobe. Things had taken a turn from innocent to sexy faster than the speed of night. Something about his thick chest of hair made me feel safe, like a secret hideout deep in the woods where as a child I would go to play.

I could feel it rise and fall with every breath and no matter how hard I tried, I couldn't stop dreaming about sucking on his nips. He was mid-sentence when I slowly closed the book and met his gaze. His lips curved into a smile, "No more story time?"

I shook my head and stood. There I was in my room with the neon lights of the motor lodge sign painting hues of rainbow across my porcelain flesh. He followed along to the bed where I sat down and pressed my cheek against his abs. He was silent as I closed my eyes and took in the musky scent of his skin. He hummed with delight, "Such a sweet boy..."

I pulled away slightly, then turned my gaze upward, where he met it with compassion beyond anything I've ever seen. Slowly he lowered his face to mine. I closed my eyes and opened my lips; I was beyond ready to feel his lips and swallow his breath like someone suffocating. Honestly, I was suffocating... dying to be his sweet boy. As hard as I tried inside to deny I needed one, the truth was I did. I needed a daddy... not just any daddy... I needed Jack. I needed him like oxygen and without him, I wasn't sure how I was going to make it.

As I was still trying to compose myself, I sat there gulping and wiping away sweat. The sound of someone knocking prompted me to jump. "Steven! Steven... are you home?"

I cautiously approached and peered through the peephole. It was Jack, and he was only half-dressed. I unlocked the door and opened it with an expression of worry and surprise. "Jack... what are doing here this late? Where were you today? I looked for you all day, and you didn't come."

He looked drunk and disheveled, but I didn't smell any alcohol on him. He licked his lips and replied hoarsely, "I got busy today, and I couldn't get away. I thought of you all day and I just couldn't get here. I'm so sorry for not coming earlier and now coming by so late, but I couldn't take it anymore."

"Take what... oh, come on in."

I sat on the edge of the bed as he stepped inside and glanced around, "This place isn't nearly as bad as I thought it would be."

I smiled and glanced at the room, "It's okay... beats sleeping in a tent or under a bridge somewhere."

"That's true," he nodded.

I stood and approached the mini-fridge, "Can I get you something to drink?"

He shook his head. I grabbed a bottle of water and returned to my spot at the end of the bed. "Have a seat," I gestured.

He did as I said, but I could tell he was a bundle of nerves. I took a sip of my water, then turned my attention back to him, "Now, what is it that you wanted to talk about?"

He met my gaze, "Steven, since the first day I saw you, I couldn't deny that you were the most beautiful boy I've ever seen."

I felt my cheeks warm as I turned my gaze away, "Aw, you're just saying that."

"No," his tone escalated, "I mean it. Since that day, I can't sleep, I can't eat, I can't think of anything but you."

I sighed, and turned my eyes back to him, "But, why me? I'm not anybody special… just a stock boy."

He exhaled and placed his hand on my knee, "You are so much more than a stock boy, you're an angel."

I closed my eyes, "Well… I don't know what to

say." I opened them again, "I feel the same way about you. I haven't been able to stop thinking about you as well."

His expression immediately turned from serious to delighted. With a firm pat to my thigh, his tone escalated with his excitement, "You don't know how relieved I am to know that."

"Why's that?"

He rubbed his neck, "Several things. The first I guess is we really don't know all that much about each other... other than there's something here that we both can feel."

I shrugged, "Well, tell me something about yourself."

He took a deep breath and turned his gaze to the floor, "Well... for starters, I was married."

"You were married?" He flashed a grin and glanced away again before nodding.

"To a woman?"

"Yep."

"Excuse my ignorance, but if you like guys why'd you marry a lady?"

He thought for a moment, "I guess I was still trying to figure out who I was. It wasn't so easy to be out back then. A lot of guys my age just ignored their real feelings and did what they thought society expected of them?"

I frowned, "No one should ever make you feel bad for liking something."

"True," he chuckled.

"Seems to me that it's not so hard to know whether you like something or not."

He shifted next to me as his eyes danced nervously, "You know, you have a great knack for clarity. You just tell it like is and don't worry whether it makes someone uncomfortable... I like that in a person."

I smiled and focused my attention on the curtain blowing in the wind, "Well, I'm just a simple boy. I am who I am. I don't try to be anything I'm not. I like what I like, and if someone says something I don't agree with I let them know."

Silence lingered for a moment before his eyes met mine and locked, "What do you think about hanging out with guys like me?"

"What do ya mean?"

He took a deep breath, "I guess... I mean... older guys."

A faint smile formed on my lips as I nervously placed my hand on his knee, "I like it, I like it a lot."

He held me in his gaze for a moment as my hand drifted further up his thigh. "Steven?"

"Yeah?"

"Forgive me if I'm out of line, but there's something I can't get off my mind."

"What's that?"

He swallowed hard, "Since we've met I can't stop thinking about one thing. As I said, it keeps me up at night and distracts me during the day?"

I turned my gaze downward, "I think I have an idea what it is."

I lifted my gaze to find his eyes looking forlorn and heavy. He licked his lips, "I understand if the answer is no, but I have to know if your lips taste as sweet as they look."

I licked them and mumbled, "Why don't kiss them and find out?"

Slowly he extended his arm and delicately held my chin. Everything seemed to move in slow motion as his lips got closer and closer to mine. His parted slightly, as did mine and I could feel all the muscles in my body go limp. I could already feel his breath and the wispiness of his five o'clock shadow on my upper lip and cheek. His lips looked so hungry and swollen. This was it, the moment I got to find out how sweet daddy kisses felt. It didn't matter that he was twenty years older than me. All that mattered was he made me feel so good. He made me feel loved. He made me feel special... like I was somebody.

To him, I wasn't just some white trash kid working at a grocery store to get by. To him, I was a person... that I mattered... that I was beautiful... that I was and am still just a little boy who wants to make his daddy proud. I never got that chance with my real dad, but maybe I can with Jack. He's a good man, so understanding and kind. He's successful and charming and funny and maybe if I play my cards right, he can save me from this less than glamourous life.

I kept expecting more pressure as his lips lingered on mine, but what he lacked in force he made up for in allure. He made me want it more. He had me squirming in my seat wishing he'd sweep me away in a storm of tumultuous lust. I wanted him to take me to the brink of ecstasy until I was shouting, "More daddy... more... please don't stop daddy... make me your little whore."

Further, we drifted back onto the dated bedspread in my room. Typically, people don't live in hotel rooms, but it was the best I could do with the little bit I made at Grable's Grocery. Our surroundings didn't seem to matter though. All that mattered was the glowing embers of what we had between us had now erupted into a flame... a flame of passion that I expected couldn't be extinguished by any means natural. Our two worlds had become one at last, and they were on fire.

They were burning with the heat of a thousand suns, and the only prayer we had of cooling it down now was for us to consummate our relationship by making it rain. Making it rains showers of love and cum. Inside of us... all over us... and all over everything around us. I want to drown in a tawdry sea of unbridled passion and lust unparalleled to anything either of us has ever felt before. Then, when it's all over and we're gasping for air, I want to go again... and again... and again. All as I shout, "Breed me, daddy! Breed my tight little hole! Breed me until I'm full and there's no room for anything more."

We were getting lost in holding and kissing when I stopped and he whispered, "Did I do something wrong?"

I shook my head and mumbled, "No, there's just something I really need to tell you before this goes too far."

"Anything," he exhaled.

I met his gaze, "Sometimes, I feel like a little boy, and most of my fantasies involve having sex with an older guy who I call daddy."

He bit his bottom lip, "You can call me daddy if you want."

"Really?" I squeaked.

He nodded with a smile, as I threw my arms around him. We rolled to one side, then the other, until he was on top and staring down at me, "So, you want to be daddy's little boy?"

"More than anything," I exhaled.

"Mmm…" he hummed, "Such a sweet little boy."

My cock was about to bust through the fly of my underwear as his butt sat heavily on my crotch. All of my senses were alive, but I was dying inside. Before, when I had sex with somebody it was emotionless. It felt good, but there was no spark. We were just going through the motions with only one eventual goal. However, this… this was different. He made me feel appreciated, not just wanted. Anyone can want someone, but to actually make them feel, goes beyond the norm. In between kisses, he lifted slightly and smirked, "Don't be in such a hurry, little one. Half the fun of the ride is the build-up of adrenaline and excitement."

I nodded and attempted to slow my breaths. There we were, body to body and skin to skin, just gazing into one another's eyes and breathing. His was smooth and patient. Mine was slow but bumpy. With his finger, he pushed my hair back then kissed my nose, "Are you going to be a good boy for daddy, let him take his time?"

I nodded quickly and closed my eyes. He called me little one and called himself daddy. Every atom of my being was raging for him to pick up the pace. I knew if I could control myself, this would be the best sex I've ever had. The only problem was when it was all over, I knew I'd be addicted. Addicted to his touch... his kiss... his big warm arms wrapped around my little body.

We started to kiss again. Little slow lingering kisses that sucked the life out of me. Eventually, he moved to my neck. I dug my fingers into his back and let out an agonizing moan of pleasure when hit that spot the made me weak. He didn't stop despite my pleasure or pain, he just kept working his way lower... worshipping my body and indulging in the sweet taste of my skin.

When he approached my cock, I gave my hips a gentle lift and he slid my undies off. He was fondling it, running his fingers slowly up and down every inch in an attempt to get me to pre-come more. I did. He glanced up and chuckled, "You're so excited. You want daddy to suck your lollipop."

"Yes... please," I whimpered.

He hummed with delight then enveloped the head with his lips. "Oh, God." I threw my head back and whined, "It feels so good."

"Mm-hmm," he hummed as he slowly bobbed up and down.

I had my hands gently resting on his shoulder as his pace quickened. For a moment, he stopped and pulled away, "I want your cum."

He went back at it and continued with a faster pace. I was clinching my ass and all the muscles in my thighs. I wanted this more than I'd wanted anything in my life. With each pass, I could feel the pressure building in my balls. I was going to blow any second. Then, he stopped and whispered, "Are you going to come for daddy?"

I nodded silently and bit my bottom lip. "Give it to me," he whispered again. From deep within my gut, a rolling whimper mixed with a grunt pushed its way from my mouth. I turned my gaze downward and sighed, "I'm gonna do it, daddy. I'm gonna come."

About that time, a stream of love erupted and rained down on my abs. Jack was growling, "Oh yeah, that's it, baby boy. Keep going."

I thought I was all out and giggled as he kept stroking me. My whole body was convulsing when suddenly everything stopped and I whimpered, "I'm coming again."

I'd never had a double orgasm before, but dear

God it was intense. My cock was on fire as another few spurts shot out and he lapped them up. I had nothing left after three times in one evening, I just layed there covered in cum and sweat when he flopped over to my side. "That was everything and more than I thought it would be."

I chuckled and turned to meet his lips in a kiss. As I pulled away, I whispered, "thank you," and he wrapped me in a hug. I rested the side of my head on his chest as he caught his breath and crooned, "Such a good boy."

Afterward, I stood and made my way to the bathroom to get a towel. From inside, I shouted, "Do you want me to help you?"

"I'm good," he replied.

I stepped out and pouted, "But I want you to feel good too."

"In time," he sighed.

Then he stood to adjust his clothes. "Are you leaving?"

He smiled, "I better get back home since you have work tomorrow."

I approached and threw my arms around him, "You don't have to."

He remained silent as I pulled away and met his gaze, "Why don't you spend the night? You can head back to your house in the morning."

He thought for a moment, then tousled my hair, "Okay, I'll stay... that is if you don't mind."

"Of course, I don't mind," I smiled, "It'll be nice to not have to sleep alone."

"I feel the same way," he replied with a kiss to my lips.

It only took him a minute to strip down to his boxers. I was already in bed waiting for him. He seemed a little nervous but excited to be with somebody. As he settled in, I moved in closer and found the perfect spot underneath his arm. "You got plenty of covers?"

"Yeah."

"Do you need another pillow or anything?"

"This is fine, honestly."

Silence lingered for a minute, before he broke it, "You know, I haven't slept with anyone in a long time. I mean... not sex-wise, just sleep."

"Why's that?"

He took a breath, "Even when I was married, my wife I slept in different beds, with the exception of a few congregate visits. She preferred it that way."

"That's kind of cold."

"You're telling me. It was one of the saddest things about our marriage. Here I was in a relationship I didn't even want to be in, and the woman couldn't even share a bed with me."

"That's really strange."

He chuckled, "It really is. But you know, I shouldn't be looking at the past. There's no reason to reach back and talk about all the things that hurt me."

"Right, we should focus on the here and now."

"Right."

Silence lingered again before I broke it this time.

"You're so warm."

"So are you," he purred.

"Are you sure you don't want me to help you take care of anything?"

"Maybe tomorrow," he mumbled.

"Okay then. Goodnight… daddy."

"Goodnight, kiddo."

THREE

JACK

In the morning, I awoke to the sound of the shower running in the bathroom. Steven's tighty whities were lying on the bed. I smiled to myself as I thought about how nice it was that I didn't sleep alone last night. The warmth on the side of the bed where his body was still lingered. It all just felt so nice. Suddenly, a stirring in my boxers prompted me to push on my wanton dick. God, it felt so good. I glanced around the room and debated on whether I had time to jerk one out before he got out of the shower.

I probably should have taken him up on his offer. Lord knows it would have felt amazing. I knew he needed to be up early for work. The last thing I wanted was for him to be worn out. Being a stock boy is no easy task. I was one myself back in the day. I still remember sneaking back to the men's room with guys for a quick blow and go when things were slow. I finally determined that he'd be a little while longer and reached for his discarded underwear. God, they smelled so good... like him. So sweet and sweaty from where he perspired during the night.

Bringing them up to my nose, I drifted my hand lower and started jacking off. Each huff of his was taking me higher and higher. Shit, I was going to blow any second. Then, the thought occurred to me that I didn't want to mess up his sheets. So, I covered my cock with his undies and creamed them. God, it felt so good to have my cock where his was. So kinky and taboo. At the sound of the water shutting off, I quickly finished cleaning up then returned the underwear to where they were.

He emerged in a cloud of steam wearing a towel, "Good morning."

"Morning, sweet boy," I replied as I sat upright.

He smiled and finished toweling off, completely oblivious to the fact he was naked. Not that it mattered anyway after what we shared last night. "You're welcome to stay as long as you'd like," he said as he reached into a chest to grab a fresh pair of jeans, undies and a shirt.

I moved to the side of the bed, "I appreciate it, but I better get back to the house. I have a couple of virtual interviews today."

"Will you come by later?"

"Of course."

I was nearly finished getting dressed as he sat down to put on his shoes. He paused for a moment, then turned his gaze to me, "It was really nice spending the night with you."

"I feel the same way," I said as I moved closer to him. He stood, then we embraced before sharing a kiss and departing ways.

In the parking lot, I looked up to find him watching me again with that forlorn expression. God, I wanted to go back up there so bad and just spend the day with him. I'd gotten a few hundred feet down the road when the phone rang.

"Jack..." The tone was cold and distant.

"K-Kate? What's up?"

"Oh, nothing, I was just going through some things at the house and found some important documents you might need."

"Like what?"

"Your birth certificate, our marriage license... which I'll just throw in the shred pile. Anyways, it's just a box of miscellaneous files and things from clients you sold cars to and other stuff like that."

"Are they mailable?"

"Not really. Anyways, Jack, I didn't call to shoot the breeze. I'm actually getting ready to head out of town to go to the beach with some of the girls. Since I'm going through there, I can just drop them by your place."

"That'll be fine, I guess."

"That is... unless there's some reason why I can't then I can mail them at your expense."

"No, you can bring them by here. That'll be fine."

"Fine... I'll call when I'm in town. It should be sometime Sunday. It's Jonesville, right?"

"Yeah."

"I don't know what would ever make you

want to move to some god-forsaken hick town like that, but it's your life."

"Maybe it hurt too much to stay where I was, Kate. Did you ever think about that?"

"No, Jack, why on earth would I know what pain feels like? It isn't like I just spent twenty years with someone who never really wanted me to begin with."

"Kate... let's not do this okay? What's done is done and we can't change any of the mistakes we made. Let's just try and move on with our lives."

There was a pause before she sighed and smacked her lips. I knew that smack. This argument wasn't over, it was just temporarily paused. In an attempt to change the subject, I asked, "So, you're going to the beach?"

"Yes, I figured it was high time for a vacation. As you know, I hadn't taken one in years."

"Well... that's good right."

"Yes, yes it is," she replied matter-of-factually.

"Then, I guess I'll just see you when you swing through town?"

"Yep."

"Alright."

"Talk to you later."

"Okay."

"Oh, and Kate?"

"Yes."

"Be careful on the road."

Silence lingered again before she finally managed to muster up a half-sincere, "Thanks, Jack."

Once we were off the phone, I sat it in the passenger's seat and blew out a breath. Kate and I hadn't spoken since the divorce. It felt kind of strange and awkward to hear her voice again and now I had to see her. It's not like I haven't heard cases of crazy ex-wives seeking revenge. Kate was never that way though. It didn't make me any less nervous. In all honesty, she was the injured party here. All the things said in the heat of battle were just said out of anger. Still, her calling me a pervert because I like younger guys crossed the line.

I'd once said I'd give her a taste of her own medicine if I ever saw her face to face again. I've recovered some, but the sting of that word still cuts to the bone. Kate was always a conservative person. Anytime she saw things on the news about LGBT people she'd just gaze at it with disgust. She was never outspoken, but what she didn't say spoke volumes... one of those silence is the same as violence type of things.

I was almost back to the house when I finally managed to snap myself out of being halfway pissed off. Even she couldn't ruin the high I'd gotten last night with Steven. He was such a good boy... so kind and sweet and considerate. I wished I'd have been able to take him up on his offer to help me, but I was just too nervous. That's the way first times always go with me, especially with someone as beautiful as him. In my previous hookups, I'd mostly just help out the person I was with and return home to jack off later.

If we were lucky enough to meet again, I would eventually loosen up enough to be able to do something. Isn't it strange how you can want something so much, but when the moment comes for you to obtain it the initial joy you expected is somehow dampened by nerves? Maybe it's just me. Some guys can jump right into kissing and making out. I've always been one to delay gratification. I want to feel them, I want to look into their eyes and experience some kind of connection beyond the physical. Up until last night, I hadn't felt that in a very long time. Yes, what Steven and I had was special, and hearing him call me daddy was getting me off so good.

I've always been a mentor, a teacher of sorts if you will. It delights me to teach these boys a thing or two and have them experience things they've never felt before. The sudden thought that Kate could never find out about Steven crossed my mind. He was the youngest I'd ever been with, and she was livid about the lawn boy who was well into his twenties... a bit older than I liked but with the looks of a seventeen-year-old. Damn... that boy had an ass like granite but the personality of a rock. Anyways, as I was saying, Kate can never find out about Steven. She'd probably report me to CPS.

STEVEN

I was as happy as a lark as I went about my daily routine at Grable's. I couldn't wait to see Jack again. What had been building between us over the past week was so exciting and special. I had high hopes that we could do things this weekend, especially on Sunday when I was off work again. Today is Friday, it would certainly be a busy one since most folks around here get paid.

On days like this, sometimes Mrs. Grable calls in an extra hand to open another register, but today she couldn't manage to get anyone. All-day, I kept glancing at the door wishing Jack would stop to pay me a visit. I hadn't been able to take a break between bagging groceries and trying to keep the store clean. By the time seven rolled around, I was bushed and more than ready to get back to my room, watch cartoons, and nap.

I know I'm too old to be watching cartoons, but they comfort and soothe my soul. When everything in the real world gets too complicated, sometimes I just regress and dream that I'm a little kid again. Unfortunately, when I got back to my room there was a note on the door from management, "You must check-out in the morning. You have broken the terms of the long-term tenant agreement and allowed another guest to stay with you overnight."

Panic started to set in, what on earth was I going to do? I couldn't afford anything else and even if I could I'd never be able to find anything within walking distance to work. For the longest time, I just sat and rocked back and forth on my bed while trying to figure out how to get everything packed and moved. The brief thought occurred to me that Mrs. Grable might let me store things in a room at the store until I could find another place.

I couldn't do that though. It isn't right to ask your boss for favors like that. Especially when she's already done so much. No, I had to be grown up and figure this out on my own. Then, like an answer to a prayer, a knock came at the door. I couldn't answer it like this. The minute I entered my room, I changed into my favorite onesie figuring I wouldn't see anyone else today.

The knock came again and I shouted, "Who is it?"

"It's Jack, kiddo!"

My heart fluttered and my mind searched for what to say. Finally, I shouted in reply, "I'm kind of not dressed for company."

"That's okay, I don't mind... I saw you naked," he added quietly.

Slowly I walked over undid the lock and opened the door. An amused smile graced his face as he saw me standing there in my fuzzy red onesie with the butt flap. "My God," he chuckled, "you look adorable."

I flashed him a sour expression of discontent as his expression grew deeper. He licked his lips and mumbled, "My God... you're so fucking cute."

Before I could reply, he dove onto me and smashed his lips against mine. My fingers dug into his back to hang on as he continued kissing me and kicked the door closed with his foot. Our tongues were whirling around like a tilt-a-whirl at a carnival as he slipped his hand into the butt flap of my onesie.

I could feel him gripping my cheek. I was whimpering and moaning as we fought to breathe.

Without a word, he pulled away and bent me over the edge of the bed. All of my problems didn't seem to matter anymore as he dropped the flap and fell to his knees. I could feel his tongue circling my hole. My eyes were closed and my face was contorting in euphoric pleasure. "Oh, yes daddy," I exhaled, "Oh yes, please don't stop."

After a few more minutes of teasing me, he stood and undid his pants. I heard them drop to the floor as he poised his big daddy cock at my little boy hole. "Oh yeah," he growled. "You're so ready for daddy aren't you?"

"Yes," I pouted, "Oh yes."

He slid it up and down my crack and bent down to whisper in my ear, "You want daddy to fuck you... make you all wet and warm inside."

"Mm-hmm."

I quickly got out of my onesie before he went any further, I wanted to be naked for him. He took off his shirt and kicked his pants to the side.

His voice was breathy as he started pushing it in, there was a lot of pain at first, but it died quickly as he pushed further inside me. "Oh yeah, daddy likes being inside his baby boy. You want him to rock you... little guy?"

"Oh, yes please... rock me, daddy. Rock me until you come. I want to fall asleep with daddy's essence inside of me."

"Fuck," he groaned.

It started slow and easy, just a gentle bob like a buoy in the ocean. Then his speed escalated and I could feel myself getting wetter with pre-cum. God, it felt so good to feel his chest hair tickling my back. As his speed increased further, he pulled me upright. My back was flat against him and his cock was balls deep inside of me. His hands changed positions. One came to rest on my belly and the other slipped around to my cock. I was dripping pre-cum as he continued pounding my butt.

Then it came, sweet kisses starting at the top of my shoulder and rising up my neck. "Are you daddy's little boy," he rasped.

"Mm-hmm."

"You ready for daddy to shoot?"

"Mm-hmm."

"Then be a good boy and give daddy a load first."

I whined as his hand began moving faster and faster on my dick. I could feel myself getting closer and closer by the second. "Ahh," I cried.

"Oh, yeah. Shoot that cum for daddy."

My breath caught in my throat. My muscles tensed to granite. He growled a moan of pleasure in my ear. Then, it all started coming out in pulses. He didn't stop though... he just kept going prompting me to squirm and writhe in his control. "Daddy's not done yet... he wants more."

Just when I thought my soul was going to leave my body, my eyes and mouth opened at the shock of another orgasmic wave rising up in my balls. I was moaning and whining like a climaxing whore as another wave of sticky love blasted into the soft cotton of my onesie laying on the bed beneath me. That must have been all he needed to send himself over the top because as he let go of my shrinking cock, he started to growl and bite down on my shoulder.

I closed my eyes and cooed in relief as wave after wave of his essence filled me to the brim then seeped out onto the floor below. When it was all over, he kissed the back of my neck and laid down on the bed covered in sweat and cum. When I rolled over, he was tugging his pants back on and trying to catch his breath. "Damn kiddo, why'd you have to look so cute?"

I grinned and replied, "I guess it was just perfect timing."

When he'd composed himself again he touched the front of my onesie and grinned, "Aw, you made a mess in your pajamas."

"It was your fault," I scowled, "I was just trying to wind down after work."

"Can you think of a better way to wind down than what we just did?"

"I suppose not."

He sat down next to me and rested his hand on my tummy, "Sorry I didn't make it by the store today."

"It's okay… we were pretty busy with it being payday and all. I wouldn't have had much time to talk like we usually do."

"Well... we're together now and that's what matters."

As he was talking, I was staring pensively at the ceiling.

"Is something wrong?"

"Huh? Oh, no I just got some bad news."

"What is it?"

"The owners of this place are kicking me out."

"What? Why?"

"Apparently one of my tattle-tale neighbors told them I had someone spend the night... which is against the rules."

"Shit, I'm sorry babe."

"It's okay," I sighed. "I'm just trying to figure out what I'm going to do."

There was a pause before he spoke again, "I have an idea... that is... if you're up to it?"

I sat up, "What is it?"

"Well..." he looked kind of shy. "I've got that big house not too far from here. You're more than welcome to stay in one of the rooms until you get on your feet."

"Really? I couldn't put you out like that."

His tone escalated, "Really! It's no trouble at all. It gets really lonely up there by myself. I would love having someone around the house... especially someone as sweet as you."

I smiled as he took my hand and I played with his fingers. "I could even pay rent."

He waved in dismissal, "I don't need your money. I just want your company."

"Well at least let me do chores or something to earn my keep."

He leaned in, "I have a lot of ways you can do that."

As he met my lips in a kiss, we wrapped our arms around each other and held for the longest time. Eventually, he broke the silence with a lovesick sigh, "You know kiddo, I'm falling pretty hard for you."

"Same here," I whispered, "It's nice to be wanted."

"Yes, yes it is."

That night we fell asleep holding and woke up in the early hours before dawn. I didn't have to be at work until ten on Saturday so it gave us time to get my room packed up. I didn't have much and what I did have fit perfectly in the trunk and backseat of his car. Even though the owners of the hotel weren't awake, I slid my key into the drop box at the night window. I guess I could have tried to stay and talk them into cutting me some slack, but I really liked the idea of staying with Jack.

This way, I could see what he was like all the time. Also, I could have daddy kisses and loving anytime I wanted. There was still something he didn't know about me that I was worried about. In fact, no one really knows that in private I'm a little boy. I enjoy nothing more than watching cartoons, laying around in my favorite onesie, playing with my toys, and coloring. I hoped it wouldn't change things between us. I don't think it will but I still worry that it might. Also, Jack was fast becoming the closest thing I've ever had to a father and I didn't want to lose that now. I couldn't lose that now.

JACK

There was something still off about Steven that I couldn't quite put my finger on. There's not a lot of guys his age who wear a onesie. I'm not knocking it by any means. In fact, it was one of the hottest things I'd ever seen. He looked so little and helpless and I just wanted to hold him close. The daddy inside of me had come to life and I just couldn't resist that beautiful body in that tight-fitting outfit.

Tomorrow, was the day Kate was supposed to drop that stuff by. I have to admit I'm pretty nervous about her seeing me shacked up with a boy already. With us getting up so early to help Steven move, I imagined he would be exhausted tonight when he got home. Hopefully, he was like me and changed into something comfortable to lounge about the house in. So, help me if he wears that onesie again, I'm going to rape his ass.

It was nearly time for me to pick him up. I turned the pot of spaghetti I had cooking down on low and grabbed my keys from the entryway table. It's amazing how excited I get, when I see him. When I was with Kate, I remember feeling so lonely. She'd always get home from work, microwave a lean cuisine, and retire to the bedroom to get on her laptop. We didn't talk like Steven and I do. Sometimes, she wouldn't even say hello.

She'd just silently fumble about the house, drop her purse and keys by the door and proceed with her daily routine. All the while, I'd go back to texting some guy on Grindr while sports played in the background. I always hated sports. She insisted that it would make me more of a man. So, to keep the peace I'd put it on. I'd much rather have been watching something on PBS or some mindless sitcom than watching a bunch of over-pumped athletes tackle each other for a ball. Occasionally, I'd find myself checking out some of the guys but after hooking up with a few, I found most of them were more repressed than I was.

All these inner thoughts were playing in my head that I didn't even realize I was in town and sitting in the parking lot of where Steven worked. He came rushing out as perky as ever and dove into the passenger's seat, "Hiya daddy, what's up?"

I flashed him a half-smile and got lost staring at his messy hair before responding. "Nothing much was just waiting for you to get off. I've got some spaghetti cooking back at the house. Oh, I forgot to ask if you like spaghetti."

"Love it," he grinned, before grabbing my hand and holding tightly to it. God, he was just so sweet. Kate never wanted to hold my hand. She always said my palms were sweaty and gross. Sometimes I needed a hand to hold just to feel some shred of human contact. Now, here I am with a boy who instinctively does it every chance he gets. I can't help but wonder sometimes if he has some kind of co-dependent personality need.

Sometimes he even seems so much younger than his age... like a little boy. I think about our first date when he seemed so grateful for that toy car, and while I was helping him pack I couldn't help but notice he had a lot of toys for a young man. On some of my porn sites, I occasionally see older boys who act like little boys. They wear onesies and roleplay with an older daddy-like figure for the sake of the show. It gets me off pretty good, especially this one particular boy who always seemed to be taking it up the ass from some brute of a guy. I wonder if some of that behavior is not just for play. Maybe there are boys who act younger than their age because it provides some kind of comfort.

I glanced at Steven and smiled. Oh boy! A sick side of my mind couldn't silence the thought of how hot it would be to make out with him while he was playing with his toys or watching cartoons. "That's sick," my mind whispered to itself as I turned to find Steven surfing the wind rushing by the car with his hand.

I swallowed hard. I had a new kink that had just been born. I wanted to be his daddy. Although, I wasn't about to confront him. Perhaps, he would tell me on his own if I made him feel safe and babied him. I finally managed to break away from my thoughts and break the silence in the car, "How was work... baby boy?"

He turned to me with awestruck eyes and bit his bottom lip. Oh, yeah. He liked that. He liked that a lot. I could feel my pants getting tighter as he replied, "It was okay... pretty busy for a Saturday. I can't wait to get home and get comfortable."

"Maybe we should watch something light to help you wind down?"

His cheeks turned red as he replied, "Y-yeah... that would be great."

"You know, sometimes I used to love watching Looney Tunes when I got off work. There was something relaxing about laughing at the silly things they do."

"I like the Nickelodeon cartoons myself like Hey Arnold and Rugrats."

"Really?"

He suddenly looked nervous, "But I haven't watched them in a long time."

"Weren't you watching cartoons the other night when I stopped by without calling?"

He stuttered as I placed my hand on his knee, "Stevie... it's okay if you like watching cartoons. To each his own I always say. Besides... I think it's adorable."

"Really?" He said sheepishly.

"Oh, yeah. In fact, it's downright sexy. Maybe you'd like to watch some while I finish making dinner tonight? Also... you could slip into that onesie and be daddy's little boy?"

"Jack," he exhaled, "I have something to tell you and I hope you don't think it's weird."

"What's that," I said as sweetly as possible.

"I like doing little boy things."

"Like little tasks and things?"

He shook his head. "Like... wearing onesies and watching cartoons, coloring, and playing with my toys."

I stopped the car just before the house and took his hand. He looked terrified as I met his gaze, "I know."

"How?"

"Well... you don't meet a lot of boys who are as sweet as you. Also, I couldn't help but notice all your toys when we were packing you up last night. Also, sometimes I see you doing the most adorable little things that remind me of a child."

"Like what?"

"Surfing the wind with your hand... playing with your fingers. It's just little subtle things that tell me you're special, your different... but in a good way."

He flashed a nervous smile, "I can't help it. I guess I just revert to habits I picked up when I was a little boy. See, when you grow up in bad situations, you find little ways to cope with the stress. I guess I just find comfort when I'm playing with my toys or watching cartoons. I used to turn them up so I couldn't hear my parents fighting."

"Oh, Stevie," I sighed. "I'm so sorry you had to deal with those things."

"It's okay," he mumbled. "I wouldn't be the person I am today if life hadn't been so hard. It made me more understanding... a little vulnerable and afraid."

"Well," I stretched out my hand and rested it on his cheek, "Daddy Jack will never let anyone or anything hurt you ever again. I promise."

His eyes welled up with tears before he buried his face in my chest, "Oh, Jack, I love you so much."

Love... the words I'd longed to hear for so long. I felt them. I felt him... every syllable as he said it. As I gently pressed my hand against his head, I whispered, "I love you too... baby boy."

He grunted with pleasure before lifting up to kiss me. "Now," I smiled, "What do you say we go home, get comfy, and watch some cartoons while we eat our spaghetti?"

"Sounds great... daddy."

Oh... he's so getting pounded tonight...

FOUR

JACK

The next morning when we awoke, we greeted one another with a groggy kiss. While he went to use the potty, as he calls it, I went to fix us breakfast. He'd requested cereal, but after a quick scan of the cabinets, I realized I didn't have any. He'd made himself comfy in the bed and turned on the TV as I peeked around the corner, "Hey kiddo, I have to run to the store to grab you some cereal. Will you be okay here for a minute while I'm gone?"

He nodded and smiled, "Yes, daddy."

I couldn't help but reply, "Be a good boy for daddy."

He smiled big, "Yes, daddy."

STEVEN

While Daddy Jack went to the store, I made my way out to the living room. I was wearing the onesie he liked and picked out a car or two to take with me while I watched cartoons. I'd just gotten settled in when a knock came at the store. The sudden thought that he was quick crossed my mind, but as I opened the door I found a lady standing there with a box in her hand. She looked a bit taken back as I opened the door and asked, "Can I help you?"

"Is Jack here," she snapped.

I shook my head, "He went to the store but he should be back in just a few minutes if you want to wait?"

She set the box down on the front porch and started to back away, "No... I don't think I will. Just tell him... never mind I'll just call."

After grabbing the box and setting it by the door, I returned to my place on the floor by the coffee table and got lost in a rerun of Arthur on PBS.

JACK

"You sick, perverted, piece of shit!"

"Excuse me?"

"What is he like twelve?"

"What the fuck are you talking about, Kate?"

"I went by your new house to drop off your box of shit and some kid answered the door in a onesie."

"Oh shit!"

"Oh, shit is right. I'm calling the cops, you pedophile!"

"NOW HOLD IT RIGHT THERE!"

Silence came across the line as I replied, "How dare you call me that! That word is reserved for people who rape kids against their will. I'm a gay man who likes younger guys but I am not a pedophile. You need to get your shit together!"

"Oh, I've got it together alright and you'll

have it together when they arrest you for shacking up with some underage boy."

"HE'S NINETEEN!"

The line went dead.

"FUCK!"

I rushed as fast as I could to get back home. Kate didn't play around when it came to things like this. If she said she was going to call the cops then she was if she hadn't already done so before calling me. I just couldn't help but think of how scared and embarrassed Steven would be if he answers the door to a cop wearing his onesie.

Unfortunately, by the time I made it home, there was already one standing at the door. I waited in the car and watched the scene from the driveway as it played out. "Son, someone called us and said you were staying with an older gentleman up here. Is that true?"

"Yes," he replied respectively, "He's my boyfriend."

"Shit," I sighed as I facepalmed myself.

The officer continued, "Well, do you have any kind of I.D. on you or anything?"

"Yes, sir, I do."

He stepped away then remerged on the porch. The officer scanned it then scanned him before mumbling, "I sure wouldn't have believed that."

"Believed what?" Steven sassed.

"That you're nineteen."

Steven snatched back his I.D. card then asked, "If there isn't anything else I can help you with, officer, then I'd like to go back to relaxing. This is my only day off."

A grin formed on my lips at his tone. The thought that if he used that tone with me I'd spank his bottom crossed my mind. Then, I secretly started thinking of ways to tick him off so I could fuel the fantasy.

Once the officer was gone, I rushed inside and shouted, "Are you okay?"

He nodded silently while staring at the T.V. then turned and smiled, "I'm great. Did they have Trix?"

I shook my head and held up the plastic bag. What do you know? I thought as I fixed him a bowl. It took balls to stand in front of a cop in a onesie and sass him. Back in the living room, I sat the bowl down in front of him and took my place on the couch behind him. I never thought I'd be the "dad" type but somehow this little twink weaseled his way into my heart and into my life.

We sat in silence for a moment, before he paused the TV and passed me a folded piece of paper. "What's this," I grinned.

"Open it," he said as he turned to face me.

As I did, I found a cut-out paper heart with the words, "I love my daddy," inscribed inside. I lifted my eyes to meet his, "Did you make this for me?"

He nodded silently as I leaned in to kiss him. "How sweet of you! I'm going to hang it on the fridge so I can see it every day!"

"Really," he squeaked.

I nodded, then tucked it into the pocket of my shirt. Who would have thought that my life would have been changed so dramatically by a blonde boy who deals in plastic bags and stocking groceries? Also, by the simple gesture of a handmade paper heart.

Love works in mysterious ways. Sometimes if you keep an open mind you might find exactly what you're looking for. We're all just weirdos anyway searching for another one we like. I know for sure I've found mine in a boy who likes to wear a onesie and watch cartoons on his day off. Regardless of that, I'm proud to say that my name is Jack. I'm a gay man who likes younger boys, and I am the stock boy's daddy.

THE END

ABOUT THE AUTHOR

Daniel Elijah Sanderfer

Daniel Elijah Sanderfer is a retired hospitality manager who lives in the Blue Ridge Mountains with his husband, William. He's written over 80 books and stories containing LGBT characters. He lives a reclusive life and when he is not  writing, he enjoy going to antique stores and taking care of his disabled husband.

Unlike other stores, Daniel likes to write stories with happy endings. Stories that inspire his readers and give them hope. To keep up with him, you can join his Facebook group Sanderfer's Socialites where he posts often about upcoming works and works in progress.

Printed in Great Britain
by Amazon

21773456R00046